The Lockdown Poems

For six- to-eleven-year-olds of all ages

by Tully Potter

The poems . . .

Most of these poems were written during the great Covid-19 Lockdown of 2020 to entertain Laila Nadarajah, now aged seven, and Anaiya Nadarajah, now aged nine.

'Onomatopoeia' came about because Laila was learning about it at school. 'The Octopus Song' was written much earlier for my friend Tom Corbett, a primary school headteacher, who wanted a poem to read out loud to his pupils. 'The Tale of Taylor and His Cat Bailey' was for one of Miriam Nadarajah's pupils, and 'Buddy's Point of View' for the Crawford children.

The illustrations and decorations are by Laila Nadarajah (front cover, pages 19 & 45), Anaiya Nadarajah (pages 7 & 41), Connor Crawford (page 37), Esmie Crawford (page 50), Rachel Triggs (page 29), Richard Burch (pages 11, 23, 34 & 40) and Haro Hodson (back cover).

Many thanks to Patrick Powell of St Breward Press, Cornwall, who designed the whole thing, put it together and cheerfully accepted all the last-minute changes.

Any proceeds from this book will go to Unicef UK.

TP

THE BALLAD OF PADDY CROTTY

Oh my name is Paddy Crotty,
I'm a tramp from Aberglotty;
My dog's a Highland Scottie
And I call her Trottie Lottie;
I'm as fat as Pavarotti*,
I look all squint and squatty,
My hair's so long and grotty
That it reaches to my botty;
My face is very spotty,
My beard is rather knotty,
My teeth are awfully rotty,
My nose is pretty snotty;
Some people say I'm dotty,
Many others think I'm potty,
So I'm off to Lanzarote
In the morning.

*A line I stole, my mind
being barren,
From my esteemed
son-in-law Karun.

THE MAN IN THE VAN

A man in a van whose name was Dan
Met a man with a pan whose name was Stan;
'May I borrow your pan, please?' Dan asked Stan.
'There's something wrong with my little white van.
'I've got to pick up my friend Anne's divan
'And help her deliver it to her Gran,
'But it's hot enough to give me a tan.'
'Oh Dan,' said Stan, 'what can we do with my pan?
'Wouldn't it be cannier to use a can?'
'But Stan,' said Dan, 'it's so hot in my van,
'And where on earth shall we find a can?
'All that I can see is your lovely blue pan.'
'That's true,' said Stan, 'we need a handyman
'Who can really make your van spick and span.'

Just then Dan caught a sight of old Nan.
'I wonder if Nan has the right sort of can?'
'Let's ask her,' said Stan. 'I know about Nan,
'And if anyone can find the best can, she can.'
'Dear Nan,' asked Dan, 'do you have a spare can?
'It's so terribly hot in my little white van.'
'Oh dear, Dan,' said Nan, 'I do have a can,
'But right now it's full of a whole lot of bran
'And I'm hoping to use it to bake a flan.
'If your van is hot, I can lend you a fan.'
'Thanks, Nan,' said Dan, 'that's a very good plan;
'We can try your fan instead of a can.'
So Nan got her fan and all three of them ran
To see if the fan would cool down the van.

'Oh no!' said Dan. 'There's a council man
'And he's giving the front of my van a scan.
'I do hope it isn't a parking ban.'
'Now, sir,' said the man, 'do you own this van?
'I've been watching it since my shift began,
'And you can't park a van for such a long span.'
'Look here,' said Dan, 'this is my friend Stan,
'Who is helping me to fix up my van;
'We were hoping this fan we borrowed from Nan
'Would cool the van in place of a can.'
'Oh no,' said the man, 'you don't need a fan,
'It's a pan you want, much more than a can;
'You can do all sorts of things with a pan.'
'May I borrow your pan, please?' Dan asked Stan.

ONOMATOPOEIA
FOR LAILA

Onomatopoeia
Was a little Greek deer
Who made some very strange sounds;
He might go Bong!
As he lolloped along,
Or Ping! as he made enormous bounds.

He lived in the woods
And loved Christmas puds
Which his mother made out of flowers;
He'd almost go Pop!
As he just couldn't stop,
Or Bang! as he'd Gobble! them for hours.

At night he would go Boom!
As he galloped through the gloom
To the sound of the owls saying To-Whoo!
He liked to sniff the sloes
But pollen up his nose
Would make him go Achoo! Achoo! Achoo!

Sometimes he would go Splat!
And fall completely flat,
Or Yelp! as he tangled up his feet;
He liked to hear Cuckoo!
Or Cock-a-doodle-doo!
But best of all he loved to hear Tweet!

If you really want to hear
A deer like Onomatopoeia
You must take care not to say Quack!
For any sort of Peep!
Like Ribbit! Oink! or Beep!
Will scare him and he'll never come back.

CECILIA SPIDER

Cecilia Spider liked to drink cider,
She said that it made her feel warm;
But people who spied her just couldn't abide her
And kicked up a terrible storm.

Young women would glare and clutch at their hair
If they found her in basin or bath;
But Cecilia was there on the way to her lair
And that was the most direct path.

With her eight hairy legs she would parcel her eggs
To carry them under her tum;
In barrels or kegs she would sup up the dregs
And end up as tight as a drum.

Though misunderstood, she was not always good,
She had eaten eight husbands at least;
She would put on her hood and lurk in a wood,
Then spring! She was that sort of beast.

Like most of her kin, she delighted to spin,
Her webs were a sight to behold;
She would welcome flies in with a sinister grin
Until they were trussed up and rolled.

At crochet and knitting she worked without quitting,
No human could call her a loafer;
When going on the scrounge, she would visit
    the lounge
And pop out from under the sofa.

She scuttled so fast that folk were aghast
And thought she would run up their sleeves;
But as they said 'Blast!', Cecilia sped past
To cuddle up under the eaves.

She felt rather sad if a mum, child or dad
Approached her all muffled and gloved;
Why so thickly clad? She wasn't *that* bad,
Cecilia just longed to be loved.

THE DRAGON WHO CRIED
FOR LAILA

Drusilla the dragon could never aspire
To roaring with anger and breathing out fire:
'I long to take part in the dragonish games,
'But then I start crying and put out the flames.'

She looked like a dragon, all slinky and scaly,
But trying to be fierce, she'd get weepy and waily;
When others were filling poor people with fears,
Drusilla would sniffle and burst into tears.

Her parents tried petrol, to make her ignite,
But dreary Drusilla just wept and took fright;
The monkeys would tease her in front of her cave,
Knowing well she would never work up a good rave.

One day a big advert came up on TV
For a promising product that might hold the key;
Could this be the answer to all of her mopes?
Drusilla was breathless and brimful of hopes.

'If you are a very dim, desperate dragon,
'You need to invest in our new improved flagon;
'It's full of the utmost astonishing oil
'Which will certainly bring any beast to the boil.'

Drusilla sent off to the online address
And shed lots of tears, making rather a mess;
She waited at home for the postman to come,

She cried and she cried and was quite damp
   and dumb.

At last in the cave mouth appeared a large box
So heavy, it seemed it was chock-full of rocks;
So trembling and sniffing, she undid the string
And there was the flagon, a most wondrous thing.

She pulled out the cork and took such a huge gulp
That it almost reduced her intestines to pulp;
She drew a deep breath, did her best not to choke
And whooshed out volcanoes of sparks, fire
   and smoke!

ADVENTURES OF DAISY

FOR ANAIYA

What can I tell you about our new cat Daisy?
She may be crazy but she certainly isn't lazy:
She tears round the garden like the
    Hildenborough Express
And everywhere she goes, she leaves a terrible mess.

She has a purr like a helicopter or a low-flying plane
And a meow that sounds as if she's really in pain.
She's the purest of white, with lovely black splodges,
And I'm afraid she is up to some dubious dodges.

She sleeps on our bed, which is the place she
    likes best
But when I want to get up, sits on my knees or
    my chest.
And when I dare to move out of my favourite chair,
Then try to return to it, guess who will be there.

When it comes to cat-robatics, she's a most
    nimble mover,
Especially when disturbed by the noise of
    the Hoover.
She thinks that scratching the furniture is
    terribly funny
And she's found the one spot in the house that
    is always sunny.

She jumps on the shelves, bringing down showers
    of things
And leaps on to the wardrobes as if she has wings.
She scatters her cat litter in all sorts of directions
And disappears if she has to go for her injections.

She enjoys a good skid on the bathroom mats
And she's even more curious than most other cats:
She likes to know what is inside the cupboards
    and drawers
And she longs to see the other sides of any locked
    doors.

She thinks my computer keyboard is for dancing on
And the piano or dinner table are really
    for prancing on.
She's sure the kitchen worktop is for sitting or
    walking on
And the back of the sofa is for slinking or
    stalking on.

She has a way of hurtling down the corridor or hall,
Usually to catch and half-kill an innocent
    ping-pong ball.
She graciously submits to being groomed with
    brush or comb:
I do hope she'll allow us to go on living in
    her home . . .

A JELLYFISH LIFE IS THE LIFE FOR ME

FOR LAILA

This jellyfish life is delectable,
I float like a big upturned saucer;
From the top I am smooth and respectable
But from underneath I am much coarser.

I'm the jelliest thing in the sea
Even though all of us look identical;
You won't want to tangle with me,
You could get badly stung by a tentacle;

The wind blows me hither and thither,
I swim with my friends in a bunch;
And I've no time to dally or dither:
I must catch something nice for my lunch.

My cousins can glow in the dark
Or parade in pink, yellow or blue;
But I like to be clear, so a shark
Will not sneak up and take a quick chew.

I dream of being orange in flavour
Or perhaps raspberry or blackcurrant;
But such fantasy doesn't find favour
When you're riding a wild ocean current.

I'm quite happy to drift with the waves,
Just pretending to be an umbrella;
So while herrings go bopping at raves,
I rotate in a slow tarantella.

Who knows where the breezes will carry me,
To Brazil or to some Eastern shore?
I may find a jelly who'll marry me
And we'll have little saucers galore…

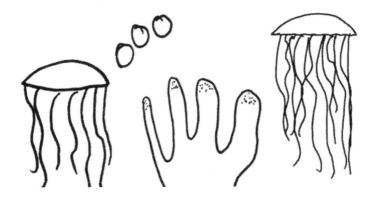

THE OCTOPUS SONG

If I were an octopus
And had lots of limbs,
I would drink eight drinks at once
And sing underwater hymns.

I'd patrol the whole seabed
Disguised as a mop
And I'd squeeze anyone
Who dared to call me a flop.

With my four leggy arms
And my four army legs
I would tickle the turtles
And steal all their eggs.

I wouldn't be scared
Of the toothy old shark,
I'd just squirt him with ink
And slink off in the dark.

SLEEPY RACCOON

A raccoon who lay down for a nap
Heard a snap! and said: 'I'm in a trap!
'It's rather alarming,
'I better look charming
'Or I'll end up as Dan'l Boone's cap.'

THE SONG OF THE NATTERJACK TOAD

Whenever it's spring, the birds love to sing
And some like to stutter in code;
But out in the pond, amphibians are fond
Of the song of the Natterjack Toad.

Chorus:

Good morning! Good morning!
It's time we were spawning,
The sun is quite high in the sky;
Each mumpole and dadpole
Must bring forth a tadpole
To fill up the ponds with small fry!

The Bullfrog says: 'Ribbit! We mustn't inhibit
'This urge to get out on the road;
'For none can be found to equal the sound
'Of the song of the Natterjack Toad.'

Chorus:

Old Grandfather Newt says: 'I have a beaut
'Of a lady to share my abode;
'We both like to dance, cavort, leap and prance
'To the song of the Natterjack Toad.'

Chorus:

The lockdown poems

A young Salamander with ardour and candour
Will add a guitar to his load;
But a strum with webbed feet is never as neat
As the song of the Natterjack Toad.

Chorus:

Battalions of Frogs in puddles and bogs
Will all of a sudden explode,
And artfully coax melodious croaks
From the song of the Natterjack Toad.

Chorus:

So let each Natterjill, in tones high and shrill,
Respond to the musical mode;
As loud serenades resound through the glades
To the song of the Natterjack Toad.

Chorus:

Good morning! Good morning!
It's time we were spawning,
The sun is quite high in the sky;
Each mumpole and dadpole
Must bring forth a tadpole
To fill up the ponds with small fry!

FURTHER ADVENTURES OF DAISY

FOR ANAIYA

Living with Daisy is one long adventure
That's come to us two late in life;
We hate to indulge in displeasure or censure
Even when she is giving us strife.

Do I want to be woken at seven o'clock
If she turns on the bedroom TV?
When I get back to bed, I'm disturbed by tick-tock
From the clock that is right next to me.

Daisy seems to believe that a window's a door
And opening it is our duty;
She will enter or leave with a wave of her paw
Like any great model or beauty.

All cats like to flourish their fine furry tail
And walk with it up in the air;
But she uses hers almost like a boat's sail
As she tears about causing a scare.

She bounces as if all her feet are well rubbered,
She can go bounding round for an hour;
One moment she's up on the bathroom cupboard,
The next, she's right in the shower.

She leaps on the bureau with faith that is blind
And enthusiasm that is quite catching;

Sometimes she slips into the slim gap behind
And we hear her pathetically scratching.

If we throw down two pillows to act as a stair
In the hope she will take a quick hint,
She will grandly emerge without turning a hair
And leave us a dusty pawprint.

It's hard to be cross when she has such soft fur
And likes nothing more than a stroke;
Her innocent answer is always to purr
Which makes us feel sorry we spoke.

WILBERT THE WORM

Wilbert the Worm had caught a bad germ
And had to spend days in his bed;
'I've got a head cold, or so I've been told,'
Said Wilbert. 'I'm worn to a thread.'

'My mum recommends that you do some
    knees-bends,'
Said Cecil, a most helpful snail,
'But even your friends can't quite sort out your ends
'And decide which is head, which is tail.'

'I quite understand,' replied Wilbert. 'It's grand
'To have this long body I've got,
'But when I go slithering, I always start dithering
'And end up all tied in a knot.'

'You need a new scene,' said a stringy French bean;
'There's a hole here, just next to a sprout;
'The neighbours are nice and we're quite free
    from mice,
'Or birds who might pull you about.'

'When my bed's full of flowers I can stay here
    for hours,'
Confessed Wilbert, 'and then I feel well;
'But when they grow veg, I stay right on the edge:
'I can't stand that cabbagey smell.'

Then Silas the slug brought Wilbert a rug
Which he wrapped round his whole slimy length;
He dozed and he snoozed, he mooched and
   he mused
Until he'd recovered his strength.

I'm happy to say that the very next day,
Our Wilbert was able to wriggle;
He had a quick peep at the new compost heap
And his pals heard a wild wormy giggle.

Now Wilbert the Worm is refreshed, fit and firm,
In fine fettle to dig his flower bed;
So try not to squirm when you next see a worm
And make sure he is warm and well fed.

OLIVER OWL

Oliver Owl would let out a howl
When anyone asked him to speak;
His feathers would ruffle,
He'd snuffle and shuffle
And cringe from his tail to his beak.

'Because I have hooded, mysterious eyes,
'Everyone thinks I am ever so wise;
'But really I'm terribly, terribly silly,
'I'm useless at French, I'm appallingly dilly;

'I can't read or do any Arithmetic,
'And the thought of Geography makes me
    feel sick;
'I can't write, my name always comes out
    as "Liver",
'I can't draw or sculpt things, not even a sliver;
'In fact I confess I'm a regular dunce,
'I've never learnt History, not even once!'

Whenever the birds wanted someone to teach
The sparrows and robins, he'd let out a screech
And say that he just couldn't make any speech;
In vain did the others appeal and beseech.

One day all the crows made a fearful kerfuffle!
Did Oliver ruffle and let out a snuffle?
No! He drew himself up to his ultimate height
Saying: 'Push off, you crows! Get out of my sight!
'We don't want you here with your
    rumbustious ways
'And the same verdict goes for the magpies and jays.
'We don't like the jackdaws, we can't stand
    the rooks,
'We want to be quiet, and to read some
    good books.'

The crows flew away with a flap and a caw
And the small birds said: 'Oliver, it's you we adore!
'You claimed you did not have the gift of the gab
'But when you were needed, your eloquence
    was fab.
'We want you as President – you're not a twit.
'You can chair all our meetings with wisdom
    and wit.'

And Oliver fluffed out his feathers with pride,
He stood tall and moved his great head side to side,
Then said: 'Friends, your offer's too kind to refuse!
'I'll be a good chairman and not hoot or snooze.'

THE MOON MAN SPEAKS

Zachary Zoon, the Man in the Moon,
Says: I like to snooze in the afternoon;
But it's ever so hard to get shut-eye
With hundreds of satellites whizzing by.

Space stations make a horrible noise
And the men inside throw away their toys;
Gadgets go orbiting round and round,
Nobody cares about where they're bound.

I can see they have garbage heaps on Earth
Miles high and even more miles in girth;
Why do they want to make Space dirty?
No wonder I'm always getting so shirty.

My beautiful Moon made of cheese and butter
Is full of the most appalling clutter:
Clapped-out old spacecraft, bits of rockets
And rubbish out of astronauts' pockets;

Moon buggies strewn all over the place,
I wish they'd take their junk back to base;
Shovels and rakes in the Sea of Tranquillity,
Rovers and modules and things marked 'Utility';

Orbiters that crashed into my garden
Without so much as a 'Please' or a 'Pardon';
Hammers and cameras chucked on to dumps,
My Moon rock smashed into lumps and clumps;

Backpacks and golf balls and dozens of boots,
Blankets, food packages, worn-out space suits;
A golden olive branch, no use to me,
Just adds to the piles of trash and debris;

They've abandoned five American flags
And all sorts of nastiness sealed up in bags;
It may well have been a giant leap for mankind
But look at what all of them left behind!

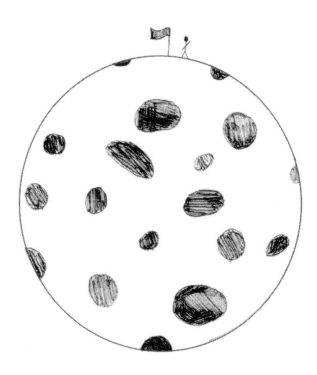

MUGWUMP THE MOLE
FOR LAILA

So what can I tell you? I'm Mugwump the Mole;
There's more to my life than just staying down
    a hole;
I work with my tunnels to aerate the soil,
I dig and I delve and I scratch and I toil.

My hands are like spades and I have double thumbs
Which may help to explain why I'm good at
    my sums;
My fur is like velvet and looks just as fine
Going backward or forward deep down in my mine.

I improve your gardens by eating the pests
Which my keen ears pick up on my
    cavernous quests;
I work through the winter along with my mate:
We're so busy, we can't stop and just hibernate.

My eyesight is weak but my strong sense of smell
Lets me know when it's spring in my
    underground cell;
I come to the surface to stick my head out
And savour the flowers with my sensitive snout.

I have other pleasures, like building a hill
From the earth that is left when I burrow and till;
I like to make sure it's a nice pleasing shape,
I'm an artist, a poet as I scrabble and scrape.

The bane of my days is Miss Priscilla Pugh,
Who hates the improvements I make to her view;
I don't like to criticise or be far too hard on her
But I really think I'm a much better gardener.

A lawn is a bore if it's nothing but green
And a molehill or two make it fit to be seen;
But to hear the laments shrieked by old
    Miss Priscilla
You'd think every one was a South of France villa.

She sends for the molecatchers, nasty old chaps
Who fill up my parlour with poison and traps;
It makes me feel queasy to see their waistcoats
All made out of moleskin – they're crueller
    than stoats.

Every now and again, though, I get my own back
When one of them comes with his traps in a sack,
Puts his foot in a molehole, gives his ankle a twist
And falls flat on his face, badly spraining his wrist.

THE MIDNIGHT YACHTSMAN

This is the tale of the midnight yachtsman:
He was an aged, bearded Scotsman;
His name was McNab, his first name Duncan,
His nose was red, his cheeks were sunken,
And I'm afraid he was rather drunken.

He wore a kilt as well as trews
And drank the most disgusting booze
Made from old bones and rusty nails
And fishes' scales and lobster tails
And brewed it all in big tin pails.

If there was any work to do,
Duncan would say: 'I'm awa the noo.'
He'd don his greasy old tweed coat
And stow some booze pails in his boat
Alongside hook and line and float.

When other fishermen took fright
Of ghouls and ghosties in the night,
And lonely foghorns sent out toots,
Duncan would laugh and say 'Och hoots!
'I'm safe in my enormous boots.

'The sea is calm, the moon is bricht
'And in a few hours we'll see the licht.'
He'd sail in his ramshackle yacht
To check his lines and lobster pot
And see what catches he had got.

One night it blew a fearful gale.
The lifeboats looked for Duncan's sail
And waited for his 'Mayday' call
As waves a dozen metres tall
Were whipped up by the wind and squall.

As morning came, they feared the worst,
They launched the biggest lifeboat first.
Surely McNab's old yacht had sunk!
But Duncan was lying in his bunk
Snoring and grunting and dead drunk!

BUDDY'S POINT OF VIEW

I'm the Four Copse Road family dog – call
    me Buddy,
I could tell you things if I could talk;
I like to go out and come home wet and muddy
Or a walk isn't really a walk.

But the proper fun starts when I have to clean up,
With Emma directing the hose;
I've loved playing with water since I was a pup,
Except when it goes up my nose.

I have to look after four children all day,
It's a very responsible job;
If some riff-raff come near, I must scare them away,
I suppose I'm a bit of a snob.

I'm a Cavapoochon, not a mere labradoodle,
My pedigree covers eight pages;
If anyone calls me a mongrel or strudel
I fly into one of my rages.

I can trace my descent from a Bichon frisé,
A bold Cavalier aristocrat
And a Poodle who used to go walking with Bizet
To help him write Carmen – beat that!

I'm told that my bark is much worse than my bite
But I'm not sure how anyone knows,

As I'm far too well bred to get into a fight
With street dogs – I don't mingle with those.

A nice caviar sausage is what I like best
With a dash of my favourite wine;
But I'll put up with chicken and eat it with zest
If I'm hungry enough when I dine.

My children are George, who's three going on four,
Then Esmie, six going on seven,
Then Connor, who's nine (he was just eight before)
And Harrison, who'll soon leave eleven.

I have to protect them from cats, rats and foxes,
I find it a bit infra dig;
I'd far rather rummage in posh dogfood boxes
Or chase Esmie's pet guinea pig.

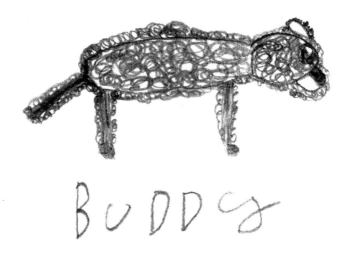

BUDDY

THE TALE OF TAYLOR AND HIS CAT BAILEY

A black-and-white cat that I know of, called Bailey,
Can be found kipping on Kyla's bed;
He likes to be cuddled by Taylor twice daily
But is fussy when he's being fed.

He won't give Purina or Whiskas three licks
And he turns up his nose at Go-Cat;
His favourite dish is a pouch of Felix
If he can't have a mouse or a rat.

He'll jump on the fridge to make utterly certain
His next meal is well on the way;
And then if it's late he'll career down a curtain
Or rattle the plates on a tray.

I'm told that, like Garfield, he's often quite lazy
But lasagne is just not his thing;
I think he would get on quite well with our Daisy
And share a quick game with some string.

He likes to go down to the pub for a beer
And a chin-wag with some of his mates,
Like Scar-Face, the tabby with only one ear,
Squint Winston, and Peg-Leg Pug Bates.

Best of all, his delight is a really fierce fight
With some of the smaller tom-boys;

The big ones are likely to give him a fright
And he's just a bit scared of cat toys.

One day he went out on a hot afternoon
And crept through a door for a sleep;
The next thing he knew, he was off to the Moon
On a rocket that kept going 'Bleep!'

The spacemen were kind, though the journey
    was far,
And gave him some tasty Moon food;
Then when he came back, everyone
    yelled 'Hurrah!'
For Bailey, the feline space dude.

Next time he has promised to take his friend Taylor:
I'm sure it will be a great trip;
Who knows? Maybe Bailey will try being a sailor
Or stow away on another space-ship!

THE TREETOP CHORUS

Around our house are lots of birds;
They throng the trees in flocks and herds.
The jackdaws sing: 'Don't be a bore.
'You've had your apple – give us the core!'

The crow sings: 'Core? There's none in store.
'I've scoffed the lot, and I want more.'
The rooks cry: 'Give us cores to gnaw
'Or we'll gang up and go to war!'

'I like to screech,' the magpie sings,
'Like a machine-gun on smart wings;
'But most of all, I like to squawk.
'Sometimes you'll even hear me talk.'

The owl sings: 'I'm quite sure of Who,
'But Why? I don't know what to do...
'And as for How, and What, and Where,
'They have me tearing out my hair.'

The pigeon croons: 'If you know Who,
'Just listen while I bill and coo.
'My mate is often asking When?
'But Which is far beyond my ken.'

'The tit sings: 'I'm a lovely blue
'And I can chatter more than you.'
The robin sighs: 'I'm all a-twitter!
'I'm trying to find a baby-sitter.'

The blackbird has a show-off song
And keeps it up the whole day long.
'I wish you'd shut up,' says the thrush.
'I can't be heard, with all your gush.'

The tiny wren sings loud and clear.
'Don't make those weird sounds in my ear,'
The sparrow blurts, 'I'm trying to chirp.'
The bittern gives a mighty burp.

The starlings make a murmuration
And take a beech tree as their station,
Then fill a whole hedge with their tweeting:
'Keep out!' they trill, 'we're in a meeting.'

'I like to sing when you're asleep,'
The nightingale says. 'Please don't cheep.
'How can I roost in all this racket?'
The woodpecker answers: 'Hack it! Hack it!'

THE TALE OF CHARLES REYNOLDS

Charles Reynolds was a dapper fox
With bushy tail and spruce black socks;
His ears were also tipped with black
And fine red fur adorned his back.

He liked to go out on the hunt
And often messed his white shirt front
With bits of mice that he had eaten:
His manners would shock Mrs Beeton.

It was his usual Sunday habit
To stalk a really nice fat rabbit:
He wouldn't eat it there and then
But drag it to his deep-dug den.

'My dear,' he'd say, 'if there is one day
'To have a good meal, it is Sunday.'
Indeed, his Vixen and their cubs
Relished a change from worms and grubs.

Among the rabbits was one buck
Named Butch, fearsome and full of pluck;
'Why should Charles kill us on a whim?'
He said, 'Let's lie in wait for him.'

Next Sunday, when sleek Charles went walking,
He hadn't time to start his stalking
When bunnies led by Butch the Warrior
Pounced, yelling: 'This will make you sorrier.'

One kicked some sand right up his nose,
Another thumped down on his toes,
And then Butch bit his bushy tail,
Till Charles fled, letting out a wail.

Nowadays Charles is a sober chap
Who every Sunday takes a nap;
While rabbits hold a jolly meeting
To boast of how he took a beating.

TALLULAH AND TARA AT THE ZOO

Tallulah and Tara, the Terrible Two,
Went with their Mummy to visit the Zoo;
They saw the gorilla
And that was a thriller
But then Tara fell in the elephant poo!

They stopped by the tigers and had a great view,
They saw all the penguins being fed with fish stew;
They saw the rhinoceros
And hippopotamus
And managed not to fall in the elephant poo!

They saw how the eagles and Harris hawks flew,
They saw birds that were red and birds that
    were blue;
They saw ducks on the lakes
And quite a few snakes.
'Look out!' Mummy cried. 'There's some
    elephant poo!'

They saw the big wildebeest, known as the gnu,
And a monkey that played on the didgeridoo;
They loved the giraffe
And had a good laugh
When a zoo keeper fell in the elephant poo!

They did all the things that most visitors do,
Like watching the owl and the kangaroo;

They saw a nice zebra
Whose name was Deborah;
Then Tallulah fell into the elephant poo!

So Mummy said: 'Now, what can I do with you?
'We'll have to spend hours in the new Ladies' loo.'
She got them all clean,
Fit to visit the Queen,
But then both of them fell in the elephant poo!

BALDRIC THE BADGER

Baldric lived deep inside a wood
And worked as hard as badgers should;
His set was full of things he'd made
But chairs were meant to be his trade.

For Baldric was a would-be bodger
Which sounds a bit like an old codger
But is the ancient woodland art
Of making chairs – yes, every part.

He'd cut down saplings in a swathe
And turn them on an old pole-lathe
To make the stretchers and the legs,
The back-spindles with their fixing pegs.

He'd shape an elm plank for the seat
And bend the back-frame with steam heat;
But when it came to the assembly
Baldric would go all hot and trembly.

His chair would look exactly right
With every joint and stretcher tight;
But while three legs did what they ought,
The fourth would be a fraction short.

The chair would wobble to and fro
And Baldric would cry out: 'Oh woe!
'My chair legs won't all touch the ground!'
His friend Hugh Hedgehog heard the sound.

'Baldric,' he said, 'come, play the man!
'You need a total change of plan.
'It's clear that chairs are not your forte,
'They always turn out rather naughty.

'You've got the skills, you've got the tools,
'Why don't you make some milking stools?
'They have three legs instead of four
'And stand up straight on any floor.'

'By Jove,' said Baldric, 'what a wheeze!
'Making three legs should be a breeze.
'Three chairs for Hugh! I mean three cheers!
'My Badger Stools should suit all rears.'

Now dairy folk throughout the land
And goatherds who still milk by hand
All use a Badger Stool by choice
And Baldric can at last rejoice.

THE NEW DAISY, DAISY*

Daisy, Daisy, give me your answer do:
I'm half crazy, all for the love of you.
It won't be a stylish marriage,
For I can't afford a carriage,
But you'd look sweet upon the seat
Of a bicycle made for two.

Michael, Michael, here is my answer too:
I can't cycle and neither I'm sure can you.
If you can't afford a carriage,
Forget about the marriage,
For I'll be blowed if I'll be stowed
On a bicycle made for two.

Daisy, Daisy, no more cream cakes for you:
It's so lazy to sit there all day and chew.
There's a lovely car in my garage
But I'll ask someone else for a marriage
Who's not so plump and likes to jump
On a bicycle made for two.

*Stanzas 1 & 2, folklore, adapted TP; Stanza 3, TP

Night, night
sleep tight . . .

Buddy